Ekaterina Trukhan

# Apples for Little Fox

Random House 🏠 New York

**Fox loved to read.**
Mystery stories were his
favorite books.

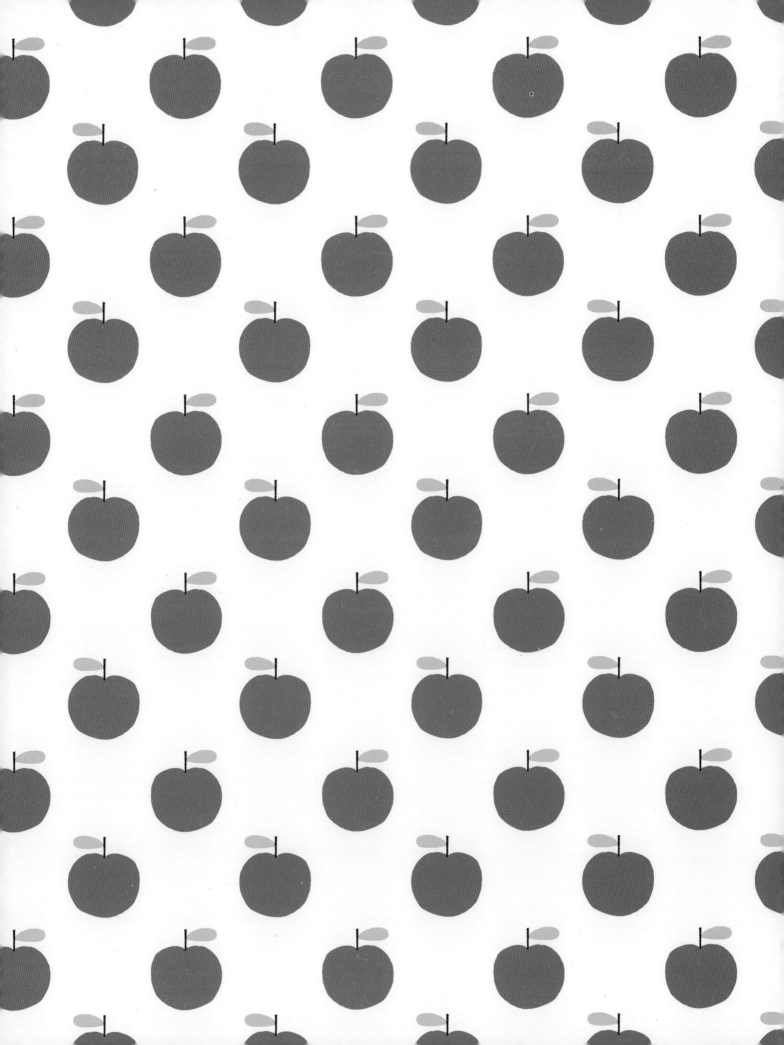

But he didn't need to investigate *that* mystery.

In the middle of the party, Fox saw that the whole apple pie had disappeared.

# HAPPY BIRTHDAY, FOX!

I forgot it was my birthday!
But now I know where all the
apples went!

Hello, Fox!

Sorry, Owl!
I'm too busy to
talk right now.

Hmm.
This is more difficult
than I thought it would be!
Maybe Rabbit can help.
He is very clever.

So Fox went to visit Rabbit.
He had just started to explain the
mystery when he smelled something . . .

sniff . . . sniff . . .

. . . something very familiar.
Something very . . . nice.

Sniff!

And there was his very favorite—
a just-baked apple pie.

Fox even questioned
a witness.

"I was asleep."

Hello, Fox!

Sorry, Wolf!
I'm too busy to
talk right now.

Then Fox looked for clues.
He used his Detecting Magnifying
Glass. He'd been waiting a long
time to use it.

Hello, Fox!

**Sorry, Bear!**
I'm too busy to
talk right now.

Fox started his investigation!
He took photographs of the
crime scene.

But when he cycled past the apple tree, just as he always did, he noticed that something had changed. **All the apples were gone!**

A mystery
for me to solve!
At last!

Good morning,
Mouse!

Early one morning, Fox set off for
the library, just as he always did.

Nothing at all.

Every night Fox wished
that something mysterious
would happen.
But nothing ever did.

Fox read all day,
eating apples . . .

. . . and imagining that,
one day, he'd solve a
mystery, too.

Good morning,
Mouse!

Fox also loved apples. Every morning
he went to the library, and on the way
home he stopped to gather apples that
had fallen under the biggest apple tree.

Fox wanted to become a famous detective, just like the ones he read about.

To those who always look for the
extraordinary in the ordinary

–E.T.

Published in the United States by Random House Children's Books,
a division of Penguin Random House LLC, New York.
Random House and the colophon are registered trademarks
of Penguin Random House LLC.
Visit us on the Web! randomhousekids.com
Educators and librarians, for a variety of teaching tools,
visit us at RHTeachersLibrarians.com

Library of Congress Cataloging-in-Publication Data is available upon request.
ISBN 978-0-399-55562-6 (trade) — ISBN 978-0-399-55563-3 (lib. bdg.) —
ISBN 978-0-399-55564-0 (ebook)

MANUFACTURED IN CHINA
10 9 8 7 6 5 4 3 2 1
First Edition

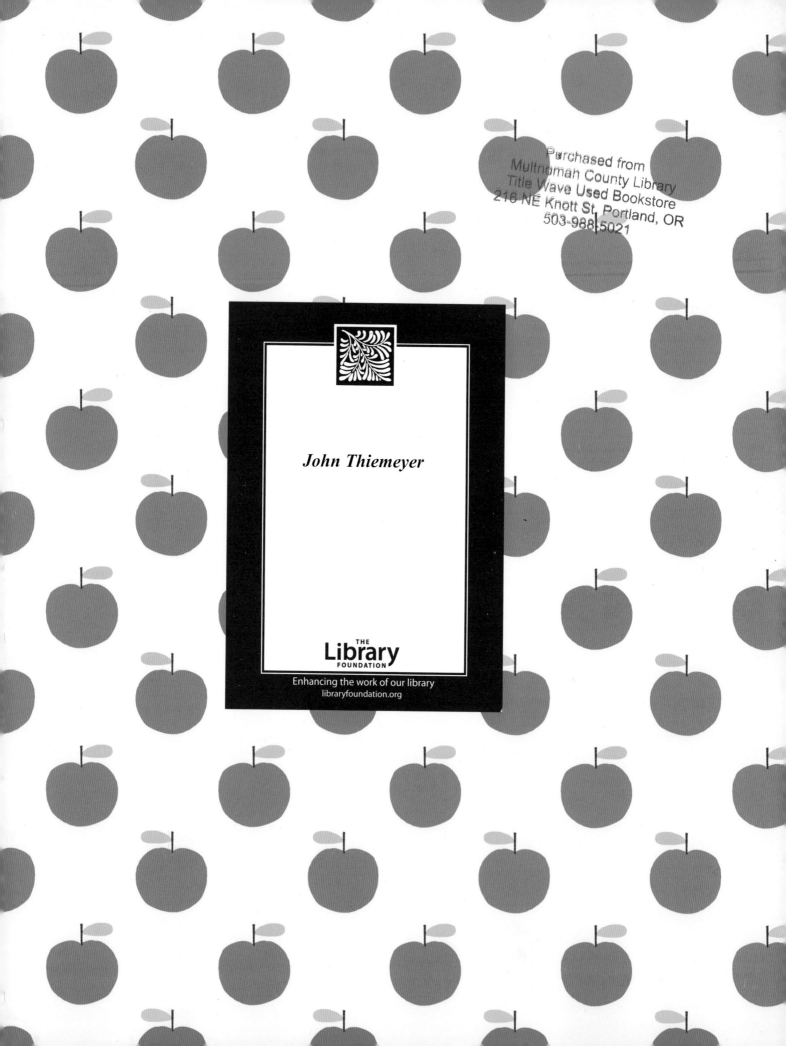

John Thiemeyer